PENGUIN YOUNG READERS LICENSES
An imprint of Penguin Random House LLC, New York

First published in Australia by Puffin Books, 2022

First published in the United States of America by Penguin Young Readers Licenses,
an imprint of Penguin Random House LLC, New York, 2023

This book is based on the TV series *Bluey*.

BLUEY ™ and BLUEY character logos ™ & © Ludo Studio Pty Ltd 2018.
Licensed by BBC Studios. BBC logo ™ & © BBC 1996.

Visit us online at penguinrandomhouse.com.

Manufactured in China

ISBN 9780593661420   10 9 8 7 6 5 4 3 2 1 HH

BLUEY

12 DAYS OF CHRISTMAS

On the **FIRST** day of Christmas,
Veranda Santa gave to me . . .
a FRUIT BAT IN a MANGO TREE.

On the **second** day of Christmas,
Veranda Santa gave to me . . .
2 magpies,

and a fruit bat in a mango tree.

On the **THIRD** day of Christmas,
Veranda Santa gave to me . . .
3 BIN CHICKENS,

2 magpies,
and a fruit bat in a mango tree.

On the **FOURTH** day of Christmas,
Veranda Santa gave to me . . .
4 GARDEN GNOMES,

3 bin chickens,
2 magpies,
and a fruit bat in a mango tree.

On the **FIFTH** day of Christmas,
Veranda Santa gave to me . . .
5 DOLLARBUCKS!

4 garden gnomes,
3 bin chickens,
2 magpies,
and a fruit bat in a mango tree.

On the **SIXTH** day of Christmas,
Veranda Santa gave to me . . .
6 FLOPPYS HATCHING,

5 dollarbucks!
4 garden gnomes,
3 bin chickens,
2 magpies,
and a fruit bat in a mango tree.

On the **seventH** day of Christmas,
Veranda Santa gave to me . . .
7 YaBBIes swimming,

6 Floppys hatching,
5 dollarbucks!
4 garden gnomes,
3 bin chickens,
2 magpies,
and a fruit bat in a mango tree.

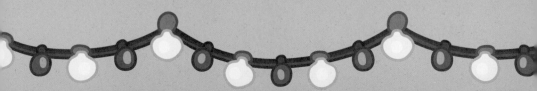

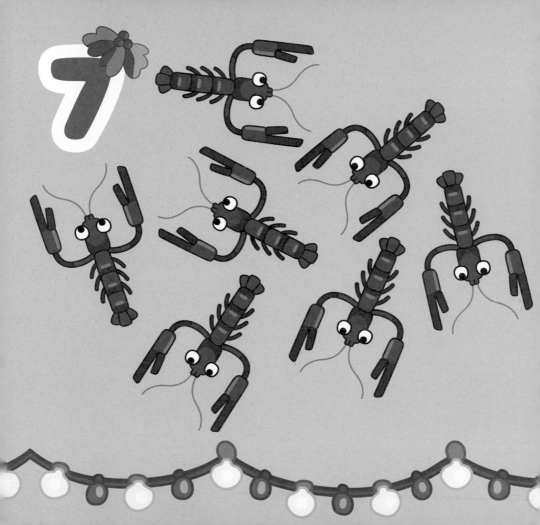

On the **EIGHTH** day of Christmas,
Veranda Santa gave to me . . .
8 LIZARDS LICKING,

7 yabbies swimming,
6 Floppys hatching,
5 dollarbucks!
4 garden gnomes,
3 bin chickens,
2 magpies,
and a fruit bat in a mango tree.

On the **NINTH** day of Christmas,
Veranda Santa gave to me . . .
9 GRANNIES FLOSSING,

8 lizards licking,
7 yabbies swimming,
6 Floppys hatching,
5 dollarbucks!
4 garden gnomes,
3 bin chickens,
2 magpies,
and a fruit bat in a mango tree.

On the **TENTH** day of Christmas,
Veranda Santa gave to me . . .
10 FROGS a-LeaPING,

9 grannies flossing,
8 lizards licking,
7 yabbies swimming,
6 Floppys hatching,
5 dollarbucks!
4 garden gnomes,
3 bin chickens,
2 magpies,
and a fruit bat in a mango tree.

On the **ELEVENTH** day of Christmas,
Veranda Santa gave to me . . .
11 BLUEYS BLOWING,

10 frogs a-leaping,
9 grannies flossing,
8 lizards licking,
7 yabbies swimming,
6 Floppys hatching,
5 dollarbucks!
4 garden gnomes,
3 bin chickens,
2 magpies,
and a fruit bat in a mango tree.

On the **TWELFTH** day of Christmas,
Veranda Santa gave to me . . .
12 BUSKERS BUSKING,

11 Blueys blowing,
10 frogs a-leaping,
9 grannies flossing,
8 lizards licking,
7 yabbies swimming,
6 Floppys hatching,
5 dollarbucks!
4 garden gnomes,
3 bin chickens,
2 magpies,
and a fruit bat in a mango tree.

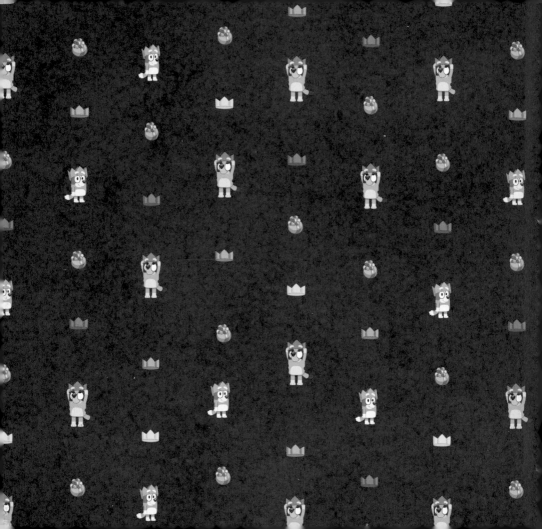